W9-BLQ-070

Sailor Song

BY NANCY JEWELL
ILLUSTRATED BY STEFANO VITALE

CLARION BOOKS / NEW YORK

For Mema, Bepa, and Barb,
and the happy years at Cove Cottage
—N.J.

Listen, my love,
and I'll sing you a song.
I'll sing you a song of the sea. . . .

Of little waves lapping
in the night,
of a watery moon-path
clear and bright,
and a sailor who's been
a long time away
now sailing his boat
toward shore.

Mama, Mama,
sing me some more.

I'll sing you a song
of a beach, my love,
of a fine and sandy beach. . . .

Where fiddler crabs scuttle
and sea grasses sway,
and a solitary figure
makes his way
across the beach and over the dunes,
whistling a sailor's homecoming tune.

Mama, Mama,
sing me some more.

I'll sing you a song
of a wood, my love,
of a forest deep and green. . . .

Of little leaves
that whisper and sigh,
of little birds sleeping
in branches high,
and a sailor who's been
a long time away
now heading down a path
toward home.

*Mama, Mama,
sing me some more.*

I'll sing you a song
of a pond, my love,
of a small and salty pond. . . .

Of ducks and geese
asleep in the reeds,
of rushes rustling
in the cool night breeze,
and a sailor crossing
an old stone bridge,
a sailor with thoughts of home.

Mama, Mama,
where is he now?

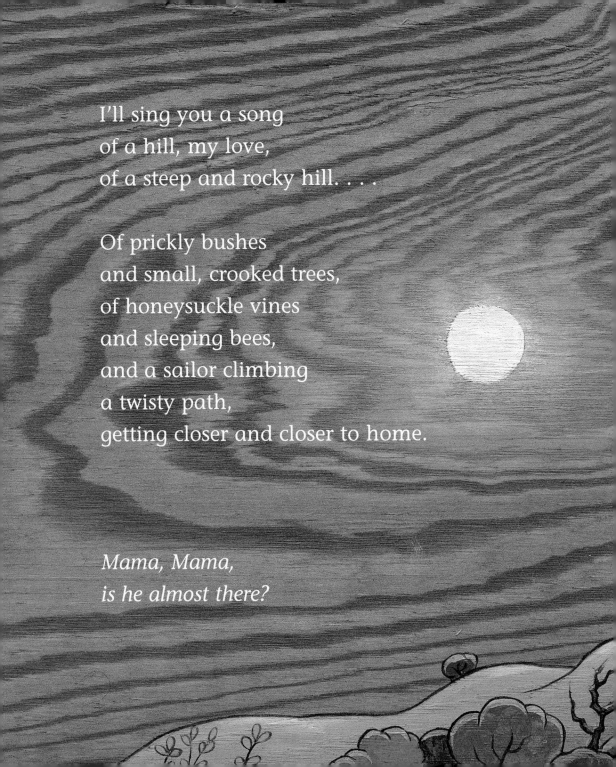

I'll sing you a song
of a hill, my love,
of a steep and rocky hill. . . .

Of prickly bushes
and small, crooked trees,
of honeysuckle vines
and sleeping bees,
and a sailor climbing
a twisty path,
getting closer and closer to home.

Mama, Mama,
is he almost there?

I'll sing you a song
of a field, my love,
of a fine and grassy field. . . .

Of the rich earth smell
that fills the night air
and gladdens the sailor
who's hurrying there.

Mama, Mama,
is he home? Is he home?

Yes, my child,
oh yes!

Now I'll sing you a song
of a house, my love,
of a snug little country house. . . .

Of the squeaks and creaks
the old house makes
as he climbs the stairs
to the child who waits . . .

The sailor who's been
a long time away
and now has come home at last.

Clarion Books, a Houghton Mifflin Company imprint.
215 Park Avenue South, New York, NY 10003.
Text copyright © 1999 by Nancy Jewell.
Illustrations copyright © 1999 by Stefano Vitale.
Type is 16-point Stone Informal. Illustrations are executed in oil paints on wooden panels.
Printed in Singapore. All rights reserved. For information about permission to reproduce
selections from this book, write to Permissions, Houghton Mifflin Company,
215 Park Avenue South, New York, NY 10003.

Library of Congress Cataloging-in-Publication Data
Jewell, Nancy. Sailor song / by Nancy Jewell ; illustrated by Stefano Vitale.   p.   cm.
Summary: A mother sings her child a song that describes how a sailor makes his way home
from the sea to his family.
ISBN: 0-395-82511-3   [1. Mother and child—Fiction. 2. Songs—Fiction. 3.
Sailors—Fiction.]
I. Vitale, Stefano, ill. II. Title.   PZ7.J5532Sai   1999   [E]—dc21   98-22086   CIP   AC
TWP   10   9   8   7   6   5   4   3   2   1